RAIN FOREST RUMBLE

BY KNIFE & PACKER

Kane Miller
A DIVISION OF EDC PUBLISHING

First American Edition 2016
Kane Miller, A Division of EDC Publishing

Text and illustrations copyright © Knife and Packer 2015
First published by Scholastic Australia, a division of Scholastic Australia Pty Limited in 2015.
This edition published under license from Scholastic Australia Pty Limited.

For information contact:
Kane Miller, A Division of EDC Publishing
P.O. Box 470663
Tulsa, OK 74147-0663
www.kanemiller.com
www.edcpub.com
www.usbornebooksandmore.com

Library of Congress Control Number: 2015938805

Manufactured by Regent Publishing Services, Hong Kong
Printed December 2015 in ShenZhen, Guangdong, China

Paperback ISBN: 978-1-61067-399-0
Hardcover ISBN: 978-1-61067-479-9

Welcome, Wheelnuts!
RAIN FOREST RUMBLE
The road ahead is dangerous! Can you handle:
Vicious Creepy-crawlies?!
Ravenous Crocodiles?!
Spooky Monkey Temples?!
If not, then turn back now!
If you can, then hold on tight and good luck!

MEET THE WHEELNUTS!

Rust Bucket 3000

UPGRADE! Extend-Legs of Legend 4

The Rust Bucket 3000 is the most high-tech robot car in the universe. Driven by super-sophisticated robots Nutz and Boltz, this team is always happy to use robo-gadgets to get ahead of the opposition.

The Wheel Deal

UPGRADE! robo fans 8

Dustin Grinner and Myley Twinkles aren't just car drivers, they are actually super-cheesy pop singers and stars of daytime TV. The Wheel Deal, their super-souped-up stretch limo, is showbiz on wheels!

Dino-Wagon

This prehistoric car is driven by the Dino-Crew—Turbo Rex and Flappy, a pterodactyl and all-around nervous passenger. Powered by an active volcano, this vehicle has a turbo boost unlike anything seen on Earth!

UPGRADE! mayhem megaphone 15

The Flying Diaper

Babies are great, but they are also gross, and nothing could be more gross than this pair. Gurgle and Burp are a duo of high-speed babies whose gas-powered Flying Diaper can go from zero to gross out in seconds!

UPGRADE!
5
supersized baby doll

The Supersonic Sparkler

Petrolnella and Dieselina (known as Nelly and Dee-Dee) are fairies with attitude, and with a sprinkling of fairy dust, the Supersonic Sparkler has a surprising turn of speed.

UPGRADE!
5
electric shock antennae

The Jumping Jalopy

This grandfather and grandson team drive a not-always-reliable 1930s Bugazzi. Although determined to win on skill alone, they are not above some "old-school cunning" to keep in the race.

UPGRADE!
10
wings of Wonder

3

CHAPTER 1

Film crews shoved photographers, minor celebrities elbowed sports stars and a huge crowd seethed. What were they all doing in the middle of a sweltering rain forest? Well, they were all there for one reason and one reason only … to watch the last "Wheelnuts! Craziest Race on Earth!"

Multibillionaire race organizer Warren "Wheelie" Wheelnut took the microphone. "A hot and sticky welcome to the ginormous, gorgeous, ridiculously *dangerous* tropical rain forest! This is the BIG ONE! The grand finale, the last race of the tournament! One team will scoop the biggest trophy yet and be crowned the ultimate WHEELNUT WINNERS!

"And because it's the final race, each car has visited the Wheelnut Garage and been fitted out with an especially ridiculous, dangerous, but mostly just downright nasty, gadget," said Wheelie.

"First up, meet the Dino-Wagon!"

Rain forest?! My backyard is worse than this place!

Our mayhem megaphone will **roar** us into the lead!

"Next, we have the Jumping Jalopy!"

We're in it to win it!

We're literally going to **take off** with our wings of wonder!

You think *this* is bad—showbiz is a *real* jungle!

"Over here, we have the Wheel Deal!"

We have a **small** surprise in store for everyone! Wait till you meet our new robo-fans!

We think this jungle course is shocking!

"Say hello to the Supersonic Sparkler!"

But not nearly as **shocking** as our electric shock antennae is!!

This environment may be unfamiliar to our computer …

"And now, the Rust Bucket 3000!"

But the Extendi-Legs of Legend will **kick** the other cars aside!

We can't wait to get hot and sweaty on this course …

"And finally, the Flying Diaper …"

And make no mistake, the supersized baby doll is not just **hot air**!

9

"The terrain will be almost impassable, the wildlife vicious, the weather filthy," chuckled Wheelie. "This is the final race so I'm going to be spicing it up EVEN MORE … with a series of red-hot surprises that will make this race the most outrageous *ever!*

"Now, I don't know about you,  but I can't wait to get started," said Wheelie as he got into position to start the race. "Good luck, Wheelnuts—there can only be one winner!"

And with that he banged a huge gong, setting off a series of animal howls in the rain forest …

VROOM!

Engines roared as the drivers blasted down the dirt track, their spinning wheels sending mud flying everywhere. The final race was underway!

The Dino-Wagon was quickly in the lead …

"This reminds me of home!" chuckled Turbo Rex as they cut across the Flying Diaper.

"This bunch should have seen the forest and mud in the Jurassic period!" cackled Flappy.

The Rust Bucket 3000 was also coping well.

"This terrain is perfect for a tank!" said Nutz.

Behind them, the Supersonic Sparkler was *not* enjoying the rain forest …

"Smelly, muddy and so unclean!" said Nelly.

"Mud EVERYWHERE!" said Dee-Dee as the Wheel Deal shot past, splattering them.

"Find a car wash, losers!" laughed cheesy pop star Dustin Grinner.

SPLAT!

CHAPTER 2

"**O**ur car wasn't really built for this kind of off-roading," said Campbell, "but I'm sure we'll get the hang of it."

"Well, I'm a bit more nervous about the 'surprises.'" said James.

The Jumping Jalopy suddenly lurched forward as Campbell found the correct gear. "Don't worry, most of the scary stuff in the rain forest will be creepy-crawlies," he said, "and they're *tiny!*"

CRONK!

GRIND!

Campbell had a bad habit of saying everything was fine just at the very moment when things went wrong! Little did he realize that as they caught up with the other racers, Warren "Wheelie" Wheelnut was looking on.

High up in a huge high-tech treehouse, Wheelie was looking through the sight of a giant laser!

"Time to spice up this race," chuckled the billionaire. "It's been far too easy so far!"

And with that, he pulled the trigger.
The jungle shook as Wheelie's laser blasted the cars. One by one they started to … shrink!

High in the trees, Wheelie gleefully watched on. "To be crowned champion of the Craziest Race on Earth should be tough," he chuckled. "And this course just got a whole lot tougher—being TINY in a rain forest is a BIG problem! As the Wheelnut teams are all about to find out!"

Being shrunk down meant that for the drivers the mini beasts were ...

HUGE!

Every poisonous spider, toxic termite and scary centipede was much bigger than the shrunken cars, and the creatures were *not* happy about their rain forest being invaded!

The Dino-Wagon had been knocked off course by a dung beetle and the Rust Bucket 3000 was in the jaws of a giant red ant.

"These beasties are terrifying!" wailed James as the Jumping Jalopy narrowly swerved past an enormous African land snail.

"It's no good, Dustin!" wailed Myley as they tried to use bad singing to get past a cockroach. "I think he may actually be enjoying our music!"

Meanwhile, the Flying Diaper was being used as a volleyball between two giant earwigs.

"Get off, nasty creepy-crawlies!" shouted Burp.

"I've had enough!" screeched Dee-Dee as the Supersonic Sparkler was engulfed by huge slimy worms. "Deploy gadget!"

CHAPTER 3

Nelly slammed her hand down on a big pink button—and with a fizz and a bang, the worms were jolted away from the Sparkler.

"I knew those upgrade Electric Shock Antennae would come in handy!" said Dee-Dee.

As the antennae crackled, the huge creepy-crawlies all sprang and slithered away as fast as they could—*they* didn't want to receive a nasty shock like the worms. The Supersonic Sparkler was soon in the lead!

As the other cars struggled to get back on course, the Supersonic Sparkler was increasing its lead, but then a creepy-crawly loomed up on them that even their Electric Shock Antennae couldn't handle—mini beasts with wings!

"Giant moths!" wailed Dee-Dee.

And there was more to come. The other Wheelnuts, who were now gaining on the Sparkler, were being swarmed by mosquitoes!

"Their stingers are bad enough when they're small," said Gurgle.

"Hey, guys—only me and Dustin are allowed to create a buzz in this rain forest!" Myley complained.

But once again, it was the prehistoric pair and the robotic duo who had vehicles built for the challenge.

"Even with those big stingers, our hides are far too thick!" laughed Turbo Rex as they zoomed past the Jumping Jalopy.

Suddenly there was a rustling in the undergrowth. The flying creepy-crawlies all fled as huge rain forest land crabs began emerging from their burrows. The crabs' giant claws soon had the tiny Wheelnut drivers cowering in their vehicles.

"Lucky we are wearing chain mail diapers," said Burp as the two baby drivers bravely faced down the advancing crabs.

Someone had to get the race back on the road and it was then that the Dino-Wagon made its move. Turbo Rex and Flappy were about to use *their* superspecial gadget!

"Time for the mayhem megaphone! We're going to need a *really* loud dinosaur!" said Flappy.

The head of a velociraptor appeared from the top of the volcano. Turbo Rex aimed the megaphone with a remote control.

"Now roar, my prehistoric beauty!" screeched Turbo Rex.

The dinosaur unleashed a jungle-shuddering roar at the land crabs. Taking steady aim, Turbo Rex was able to blast the creatures back.

"They're moving away," said Flappy. "Let's go!"

CHAPTER 4

The crabs snapped at their exhausts, but the cars had time to swerve away and the race was back on. Watching it all was Warren Wheelnut . . .

"They are a resourceful bunch," said Wheelie. "And as much as I enjoyed it, I guess it's time to change them back to their true size."

He reversed the laser mode and blasted the Wheelnuts again—back to normal size!

The cars were now driving deeper and deeper into the jungle. But one car was not worried about the road ahead—it had to make an urgent pit stop.

"We're running out of fuel," said Gurgle, pointing at the tank on the back of their car.

"Good thing we're in a rain forest," said Burp. "This is the perfect place to find our fuel source." The Flying Diaper ran on a stinking green tropical compost found at the foot of the Pong Plant!

While Gurgle and Burp are seeking out the smelliest, dingiest corner of the rain forest, let's take a closer look at their car—as we put the Flying Diaper UNDER THE SPOTLIGHT!

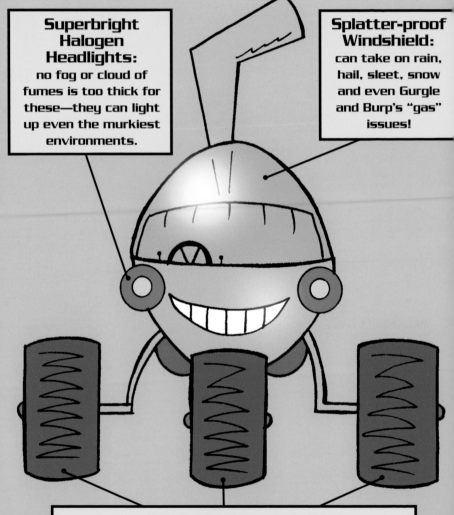

Superbright Halogen Headlights: no fog or cloud of fumes is too thick for these—they can light up even the murkiest environments.

Splatter-proof Windshield: can take on rain, hail, sleet, snow and even Gurgle and Burp's "gas" issues!

Bionic Bumper Tires: to make sure the car never tips over, these are made from toughened rubber that can take on the most horrible highways—and double up as a teething toy.

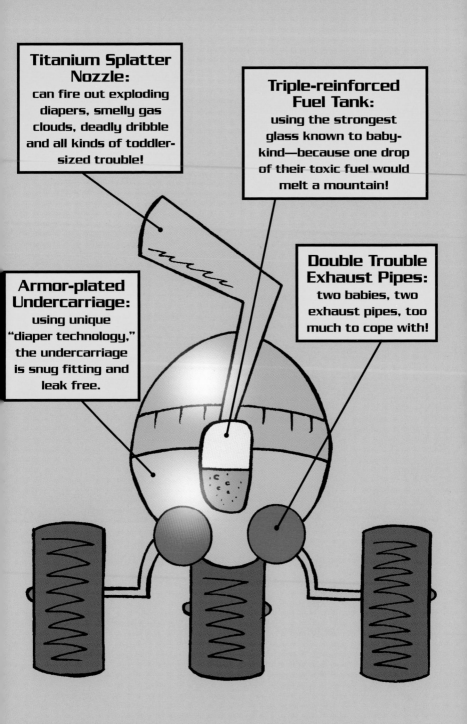

Titanium Splatter Nozzle: can fire out exploding diapers, smelly gas clouds, deadly dribble and all kinds of toddler-sized trouble!

Triple-reinforced Fuel Tank: using the strongest glass known to baby-kind—because one drop of their toxic fuel would melt a mountain!

Armor-plated Undercarriage: using unique "diaper technology," the undercarriage is snug fitting and leak free.

Double Trouble Exhaust Pipes: two babies, two exhaust pipes, too much to cope with!

Now, Gurgle and Burp could take most gross things, but even they found what lurked under the Pong Plant hard to stomach. A stinking, bubbling, green slime was giving off a stench that was super smelly!

"OK, you hold the pipe, I'll pump," said Gurgle as his eyes watered.

There was a loud and disgusting squelching noise as they filled the tank.

"Phew—now to rejoin the race," said Burp. With their tank topped up, they were soon catching up with the other racers.

CHAPTER 5

The cars had driven through an especially dense area of forest and were now on a plateau.

"This is *so* much better!" said Dustin. "Blue sky and sunshine!"

"Computer says we are clear of danger," said Nutz.

But if they thought getting away from trees was going to make the race easier, they were wrong. It wasn't long before dark shadows loomed over the course—the danger was now from above!

Huge toucans, parrots and vultures swept down to peck at the Wheelnuts. The feathered menaces were causing chaos! The Dino-Wagon had lost the lead when a particularly aggressive orange-bellied parrot landed in front of Turbo Rex, making them swerve off the road.

"Just keep your eyes on the road!" screeched Flappy.

"I can't see anything!" wailed the distraught dinosaur.

A flock of flamingos had gotten through the Wheel Deal's open sunroof and began wading in their hot tub!

"This is *so* unglamorous!" whined Dustin as he tried to scare the birds away.

Meanwhile, a family of toucans was nesting on top of the Supersonic Sparkler!

"I think the big one is going to lay an egg!" whined Dee-Dee.

But suddenly the birds all flew away.

"Can't see anything to worry about," puzzled Campbell as he swept the Jumping Jalopy to the front of the race. "Just a few feathered friends playing."

However, no sooner had he spoken than a massive, terrifying bird swooped down, forcing them to make an emergency stop.

SCREECH!

"It's a giant condor!" exclaimed James. "But its beak looks like it's made of metal!"

"Time for some old-school klaxon power," said Campbell as he honked the horn.

The huge bird eventually flapped away ... but if we take a closer look, we'll see that this is no ordinary condor. It is in fact a robot bird being flown by none other than Wipeout Wheelnut and his unpleasant sidekick, Dipstick!

Unlike his multibillionaire brother, Wheelie, Wipeout was a bit of a loser and his main aim in life was wrecking his brother's races.

"For four races I've tried to ruin my brother's competition," said Wipeout. "Well, fifth time lucky!"

"This hang glider disguised as a bird is the perfect way to spy on the racers," said Dipstick.

"Now, let us fly back to base camp to put my evil plan into action," said Wipeout. But just then, a big gust of wind picked up their glider, tossed it high into the air and dumped it with a deafening SPLAT! right in the middle of a bog!

"OK, now let us *walk* back to base camp to put my evil plan into action," said Wipeout through a mouthful of mud.

CHAPTER 6

The Flying Diaper's full tank was firing them into the lead, but the Rust Bucket 3000 and the Dino-Wagon were just behind them.

"We need something big to happen," said Nelly in the Supersonic Sparkler.

"Make that something HUGE," shouted James as the leading cars disappeared around a turn.

Fortunately, Wheelie certainly had something BIG in store for the Rain Forest Rumble race. Actually, make that ENORMOUS! The drivers were about to encounter the jungle's heavyweights and no car was going to come through unscathed!

The Flying Diaper bumped into something large and leathery—an elephant!

A rhino butted the Rust Bucket 3000 onto its back!

The Dino-Wagon was cornered by a huge buffalo!

An enormous brown bear sat grumpily on the hood of the Jumping Jalopy!

A giant three-toed sloth was slowly squeezing the Supersonic Sparkler!

At the very back of the track, a jaguar was growling scarily at the Wheel Deal!

Just as Wheelie had hoped, the large jungle animals were creating chaos. Was this the end of the race? It might have been, had one of the crews not quickly decided to deploy their gadget.

"Time to unleash our Army of Fans!" said Dustin.

"Fans?! In the middle of a jungle?" said James as the huge bear licked its lips.

"Not *real fan*s," said Myley. "It's time to unleash the ROBO FANS!"

The trunk of the car popped open and out sprang an army of tiny robotic fans!

"WE LOVE MYLEY! WE LOVE DUSTIN!" chanted the robo fans.

"Then spread the love!" squealed Myley. "Scare off that big pussy cat!"

"OBEY MYLEY! OBEY DUSTIN!" said the robo fans before they turned their attention to the jaguar. With a blood-curdling robot cry, the mini fans swarmed around it. The toothy feline wisely decided that it was time to back off and it quickly fled. The showbiz duo were back in the race!

As they sped off, they realized that their mini fans were now frightening off *all* the wildlife.

"That's enough!" said Dustin. "Stop helping the other Wheelnuts!"

But the robo fans were too good, scaring all the jungle creatures. It was too late and pretty soon the race was back on for *all* the teams!

The first checkpoint loomed into view.

"Hey, you've left your fans behind!" shouted James. But the Wheel Deal were not going to turn back for anyone, and as the line appeared, they swerved in front of the Supersonic Sparkler, who was narrowly ahead of the Flying Diaper.

CHAPTER 7

The road narrowed before passing through an ancient crumbling doorway. The drivers had reached the first checkpoint and there to meet them was Warren "Wheelie" Wheelnut himself.

The stars: 6 stars for first place, 5 stars for second place, 4 stars for third place, 3 stars for fourth place, 2 stars for fifth place and 1 star for sixth place.

SAFARI SO GOOD CHECKPOINT

1	Wheel Deal	✪✪✪✪✪✪
2	Supersonic Sparkler	✪✪✪✪✪
3	Flying Diaper	✪✪✪✪
4	Jumping Jalopy	✪✪✪
5	Dino-Wagon	✪✪
6	Rust Bucket 3000	✪

"Well done, drivers—the rain forest can make even the biggest of us feel really small," chuckled Wheelie. "Now it's time for the 'Wheelnut Challenge.' Because this is the last race, *this* one is going to be the toughest yet! Behind me is an ancient temple. Each of you will go to a separate chamber where my specially trained monkeys will make your life a misery. I call this challenge, 'Get That Monkey Off My Back!' And as always, this challenge is all about who can last longest," said Wheelie. "When you've had enough, just shout, 'I'm a Wheelnut, get me out of here!'"

Each team nervously entered stone chambers with their names carved over the doorways. Suddenly, the temple shook as high-pitched monkey howls echoed through the creepy old building …

Monkeys scampered into the chamber of the Supersonic Sparkler. They were the grossest, smelliest monkeys ever!

In the next chamber along, the Rust Bucket 3000 was visited by the noisiest monkeys ever—they made a racket so loud and high-pitched, it was affecting the robots' circuits!

The Jumping Jalopy's monkeys were armed with blowpipes!

The Dino-Wagon crew were wondering what was going to happen to them, when a particularly large monkey appeared carrying a big stick, which Flappy and Turbo Rex quickly recognized.

It was time for the Wheel Deal to meet *their* monkeys. Into their chamber scampered a pop group made up of monkeys and they couldn't play a single note!

That left the Flying Diaper crew. Could the babies outlast their fellow Wheelnuts? Clown monkeys appeared—and they were armed! But they were no match for Gurgle and Burp.

With a jungle-shaking BURP, it was the monkeys who couldn't take any more. They fled as quickly as their hairy little legs could carry them.

"Congratulations, Flying Diaper—you won the Challenge!" said Wheelie. "That's **5 bonus Gold Stars!** Now it's time to get back to the race."

CHAPTER 8

But as we've learned, things are never straight-forward in a Wheelnuts race!

"I don't want to *dampen* your spirits, or *rain* on your parades, but things are going to get a little, er, how should I say … 'wet,'" said Wheelie as he stood next to a control panel.

"Our computer does not indicate any imminent rainfall," said Nutz.

But the ground beneath the Wheelnuts began to shake and shudder as Wheelie pulled a large lever.

"Is it me, or are we sliding downward?" said Flappy.

"The last time I had this feeling was when our greatest hits album slipped down the charts," said Dustin.

Their cars had been put on rafts and they were being tipped into a raging river!

As the rafts careened through the water, the Flying Diaper shot to the front as it swerved past the other drivers, covering them in spray.

"All we need is a rubber ducky and this is like the best bath time ever!" chortled Burp.

"Hey! That has *so* ruined my hairstyle!" screeched Dustin, who had been water-skiing behind the Wheel Deal car.

Meanwhile, the Dino-Wagon was now lurching towards the side of its raft!

"Heave!" said Flappy as Turbo Rex tried to pull their car back on board. "We've got a race to win!"

Behind the race leaders, the other cars were finding the conditions *really* tough.

"I can see an eel nibbling the underside of the raft!" wailed Dee-Dee.

The Rust Bucket 3000 had completely lost control and was swirling around and around in a whirlpool! Only the Jumping Jalopy was making any headway.

"I knew my white-water rafting experience would come in handy!" said James as he took the inside line on a turn to get past the Supersonic Sparkler and the Rust Bucket 3000.

But as the race thundered on, the drivers became aware of a loud roaring noise. "Hold on tight!" said Gurgle as the rafts began to spin out of control.

"There must be a way to slow down!" said Boltz as he madly jabbed buttons.

"Can we just pull over and have a time-out?" said Myley as she held the steering wheel as tightly as she could.

But there was no slowing down and no pulling over, because the Wheelnuts were about to be flung over the edge of a massive …

WATERFALL!!!

The Wheelnuts clung to whatever was at hand as they tumbled through the air. There were wheels, helmets and rafts everywhere and a loud screeching echoed across the rain forest!

With a series of loud splashes, the Wheelnuts hit the water beneath the waterfall. One by one, the rafts bobbed back up to the surface.

"I'm wetter than a platypus's pajamas," said Campbell, wringing out his moustache.

But there was no time to worry about being wet. The race was back on—*across a lake!*

In the distance, the drivers could just make out where the road started again. All that stood between them was a stretch of crystal clear lake.

"We just need to get across and we can ditch these silly rafts," said Dee-Dee as the Supersonic Sparkler took the lead.

"There's nothing to worry about here," said Campbell as the Jumping Jalopy raced on.

But no sooner did the drivers reach the middle of the lake than it became clear they were not alone.

"I think something big and green with lots of teeth is gnawing the back of our raft!" quivered Dustin.

"Crocodiles!!!" shouted James.

"COMPUTER SAYS DANGER! COMPUTER SAYS DANGER!" wailed Nutz.

Panic set in as the crocodiles began chomping the Wheelnuts' rafts out from under them, but even worse was to come … hippopotamuses were now blocking the route to shore!

"Well, we enjoyed the race while it lasted," said Turbo Rex. "But I can't see any way out of this."

But as is so often the case in a Wheelnuts race, when the going gets tough, the tough get *cheating!*

"Time to kick those other drivers aside!" said Nutz. "Reveal the Extendi-Legs of Legend!"

Two small panels on the Rust Bucket 3000 slid apart and a huge pair of robot legs appeared. The vehicle rose above the surface of the water—it was now standing on the bottom of the lake!

"Forward, MARCH!" shouted Boltz.

The Rust Bucket 3000 could now stride across the lake, and there was nothing the wildlife below could do but look on in amazement.

"Snap all you like, Mr. Crocodile, but winning this race is like a walk in the park!" chuckled Nutz.

There was just one small problem—the wildlife was so distracted by the spectacle that the other drivers were making progress too.

"As soon as we get onto dry land, we have to get motoring!" said Boltz.

CHAPTER 9

Unfortunately, as soon as the Rust Bucket 3000 reached dry land, their robot legs got tangled up in some weeds and the other drivers were hot on their heels!

One by one, the drivers' rafts made it across the lake, and after a final snap at the Dino-Wagon's volcano from a very grumpy crocodile, the competitors were back on solid ground.

"Surely the race can't get any harder," said Dee-Dee as the drivers entered increasingly thick rain forest on the drive up into the hills.

Not only was the terrain getting tougher ... the drivers were once again being watched by the huge condor they'd encountered earlier.

"They are perfectly placed for my little 'surprise,'" cackled the villainous Wipeout Wheelnut.

"Time to cause a little rumble in the jungle!" said Dipstick, handing his boss a remote control.

With a final cackle, Wipeout pressed a button on the control panel. At first, nothing happened ... but then there was a series of loud explosions!

The Wheelnuts all shook and wobbled as the explosions rumbled in the hills behind them.

"Hopefully there isn't a rainstorm coming," said Flappy. "Our tires can't take any more mud."

"Is it me, or is the ground shaking?" said Dustin.

The ground was indeed shaking. Just as Wipeout had planned, his detonations had set off a landslide. The Wheelnuts were being swept spinning and plummeting down the mountain in a giant jumble of earth, trees and debris!

It was a case of holding on as the cars tumbled down the hill.

"Wait until they see what I have in store for them at the bottom!" howled Wipeout.

"A sticky welcome, with strings attached!" added Dipstick.

As he spoke, the drivers tumbled over the edge of the mountain into a HUGE spider's web!

CHAPTER 10

One after another, the Wheelnuts splatted into the spider's giant web and couldn't move, no matter how hard they tried!

As the drivers struggled, there was a loud crash in the forest and a huge head appeared.

"That thing is like no spider I have ever seen before," said Campbell.

"If it *is* a spider," exclaimed James.

"Computer says artificial life form," said Boltz as he frantically tried to find out what they were up against.

"Hey! That's just *so* not glitzy," said Myley as she spotted a glint from the top of the creature. "It's some sort of car ... being driven by Wipeout!"

"There's a new Wheelnut in town, you miserable motorists—meet the Spidomatic!" cried Wipeout as he trundled into view.

"And with you all being a little 'tied up,' I, the wonderfully wicked Wipeout Wheelnut, will win the race!"

"And then destroy it forever!" added Dipstick.

Wipeout's robotic spider car now took aim. The Wheelnuts were about to be caught in its woeful web!

It was time for some teamwork, and Nelly had a plan.

Because their car was shaped like a butterfly, the Supersonic Sparkler crew had an idea how to out-creepy-crawly a creepy-crawly!

"We're going to have to trap the trapper," said Nelly. "Let me explain …"

The drivers all quickly climbed down from their vehicles. Once on the ground, it was time to execute Nelly's plan.

The first thing to do was create a distraction, and it was Dustin and Myley who were tasked with getting the giant spider's attention.

With the spider distracted, it was time to attack—Gurgle and Burp formed a catapult from a diaper …

Then the strongest and most mechanically minded Wheelnuts, Turbo Rex and Campbell, were catapulted onto the top of the spider!

Turbo Rex pulled open the metal hood, revealing the engine that was powering the giant arthropod …

Next up, Campbell used his engine know-how to readjust the engine so that the spider started motoring around in a circle!

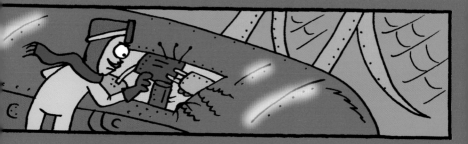

"What is going on?!" wailed Wipeout. "Why is my spider going all freaky?!"

"I can't stop it, sir," said Dipstick as he desperately tried to get the eight-legged monster to go in a straight line. But the Wheelnuts weren't finished—the Rust Bucket 3000 used their grabbing arm to heave a large rock into position and as soon as the spider clambered onto it, it flipped the rock over so that the spider was stuck underneath!

"You won't be seeing the checkered flag in *this* race!" chuckled Campbell.

THUNK!

CHAPTER 12

The Wheelnuts quickly hacked their cars free from the sticky web and the race was back on! The Jumping Jalopy was soon right on course as the road started to head upward …

"This is like no road I have ever seen before," said Campbell as the track left the ground and swept up to the top of the trees.

"It's like a hanging walkway built for cars," said James as he looked down at the sheer drop on either side of them. Not only was the track scary— within seconds they were being stalked by mean-looking gorillas, gibbons and apes!

With the final checkpoint in sight, the drivers were racing with a newfound intensity. Up front, the Wheel Deal had taken the lead and Dustin was belting out a song that was scaring off the monkeys.

The Rust Bucket 3000 was right behind them. Monkeys were throwing all kinds of fruit at their car—but it was all just bouncing off the super-tough metallic bodywork!

The road started winding up to the top of a vast ancient tree. In the Dino-Wagon, a triceratops appeared out of the volcano and was heading coconuts back at the apes ... but the Flying Diaper was struggling to keep up.

"Super-nasty gadget time?" said Gurgle.

"Yes, deploy the supersize baby doll!!" said Burp.

A missile flew out of the Flying Diaper and exploded—into a huge inflatable doll! It floated up high into the sky.

"Well, we've seen some exotic wildlife on this drive, but *that* is amazing!" said James.

"It's so cuuuuuuuute!" said Myley.

But the gigantic doll was there as a cheat, and as the Wheelnuts were about to discover, it may have looked big and bouncy, but it was actually quite dangerous.

"It's coming straight for us!" wailed Nelly.

"We can't get out of its way!" screeched Flappy.

WIBBLE!
WOBBLE!

As the drivers did their best to dodge the doll, the Supersonic Sparkler saw its chance and swooped through the final checkpoint to be firmly in the lead!

The stars: 6 stars for first place, 5 stars for second place, 4 stars for third place, 3 stars for fourth place, 2 stars for fifth place and 1 star for sixth place.

TREE TOP CHECKPOINT

1	Supersonic Sparkler
2	Dino-Wagon
3	Rust Bucket 3000
4	Flying Diaper
5	Wheel Deal
6	Jumping Jalopy

CHAPTER 13

The final checkpoint was a gate on a bridge that led to the top of the biggest tree any of the drivers had ever seen. The final section of the race would be on a road that ran down the tree like a long, twisting, turning giant slide!

"Spluttering spark plugs!" exclaimed Campbell. "Super steep, super-fast and super dangerous!"

With every car desperate to win, the Wheelnuts bumped, banged and clanged their way down the track.

The Wheel Deal managed to take the lead after Dustin sang a note so high that some of the fruit on the tree exploded— covering the other drivers in an icky mush!

The Dino-Wagon unleashed a prehistoric wood-pecking dinosaur that covered the road in wood chips!

The Flying Diaper briefly took the lead by swinging ahead on some vines!

The Supersonic Sparkler was hovering like a butterfly, but then Dee-Dee panicked and tipped them upside down!

The Rust Bucket 3000 used spiky caterpillar tracks for a better grip on the road!

And the Jumping Jalopy trundled along at the back ...

However, Warren "Wheelie" Wheelnut had one final trick up his sleeve—a terrifying surprise that would have a huge impact on the race.

As the drivers spun around yet again, something scaly and glistening lay across the road.

"A giant anaconda!" screeched Nelly. "The world's biggest snake!"

One by one the cars screeched to a halt.

"It's quite vile!" said Dustin. "Can't anyone move it?"

"Well, *I'm* not going anywhere near it," said Turbo Rex, eyeing the huge reptile suspiciously. "We're going to have to wait for it to move on."

But one car hadn't ground to a halt—in fact, James and Campbell were so far back that they had seen the whole incident unfold.

"Look, Grandpa, it's a disaster," said James.

"Time to deploy *our* gadget!" said Campbell defiantly. "Unfurl the Wings of Wonder!" With a press of a button, wings appeared on either side of the car and it flew clean over the snake!

"Gramps, you're a genius!" said James.

CHAPTER 14

But if the Jumping Jalopy thought they could just cruise to the finish line they were sadly mistaken.

"We don't have the power to stay in the air very long," said Campbell as he struggled to keep the car up.

"I think we're going to laaaaaaaaand!" screeched James as they crashed back down onto the road.

With smoke belching out the back of their car, the Jumping Jalopy limped towards the finish line. And as the giant snake slithered away after some tastier food, the rest of the cars were hot on their heels …

The Wheel Deal was within touching distance and the cheesy pop duo was singing every bad song in their repertoire.

The Dino-Wagon blasted a lump of volcanic rock that James whacked away with a wrench!

The Flying Diaper fired off a jungle-melting cloud of Pong Plant gas while the Supersonic Sparkler blasted a puff of their strongest fairy dust! Meanwhile, the Rust Bucket 3000 tried to grab them with their giant metal claw!

But Campbell summoned all of his driving skills and the Jumping Jalopy made it over the line in FIRST PLACE. The crowd went totally *wild!*

Final Race Placings

1 Jumping Jalopy

2 Rust Bucket 3000

3 Supersonic Sparkler

4 Flying Diaper

5 Dino-Wagon

6 Wheel Deal

The final race was over and there to meet the exhausted drivers was their race director, Warren "Wheelie" Wheelnut.

"Congratulations, Wheelnuts!" chuckled Wheelie. "You guys have raced through desert and snow, underwater and on the moon, but our final winners here in the jungle are James and Campbell—and their Jumping Jalopy!"

Just then there was a loud bang, smoke belched out of the Jumping Jalopy's engine and the wheels fell off!

"Looks like we wouldn't have lasted much longer," said James.

"Lucky it's the end of the race," said Campbell. "Looks like we all need a rest!"

While everyone catches their breath, let's take a closer look at the Jumping Jalopy—as we put the winning car UNDER THE SPOTLIGHT!

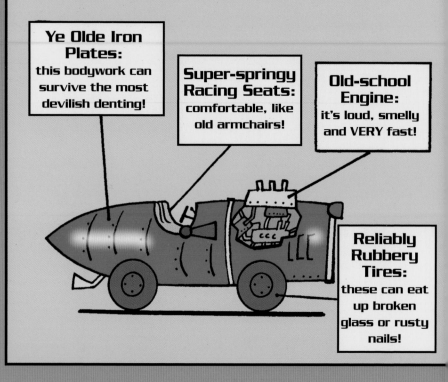

Ye Olde Iron Plates: this bodywork can survive the most devilish denting!

Super-springy Racing Seats: comfortable, like old armchairs!

Old-school Engine: it's loud, smelly and VERY fast!

Reliably Rubbery Tires: these can eat up broken glass or rusty nails!

Everyone turned to see one final car limping towards them—it was Wheelie's brother in the Spidomatic!

"My evil vehicle just isn't fast enough. I'm through with disrupting races," groaned a wiped out Wipeout.

"I think we need to find you a job," laughed Wheelie. "How about helping to organize the next Wheelnuts races?"

His defeated brother shook Wheelie's hand and managed a thin smile.

"Right! Time for trophies," said Wheelie, turning back to the crowd. "The third place Mischievous Monkey Medal goes to the Supersonic Sparkler. In second, for the Jungle Juggernaut Bowl, it's the Rust Bucket 3000. And for winning the final race, the ridiculously, absurdly HUGE Totally Tropical Trophy of Triumph goes to Campbell and James in the Jumping Jalopy!"

"But there are no losers here. To thank you *all* for making this race *such* fun—I have prepared a feast to celebrate our wonderful Wheelnuts teams."

Just then, an ice cream truck appeared.

"Yippee!" cheered the drivers.

"Of course, there are extra toppings and sauces for the racers with the most Gold Stars!" added Wheelie. "And after that," he went on, "moldy macadamia nuts, sour banana milk shakes and jellied jungle bugs for everyone!" chortled Wheelie. "Only kidding!" And with that, the first-ever Craziest Race on Earth was over.